STERLING CHILDREN'S BOOKS
New York

An Imprint of Sterling Publishing
387 Park Avenue South
New York, NY 10016

ISBN 978-1-4027-8342-5

Library of Congress Cataloging-in-Publication Data Available

Distributed in Canada by Sterling Publishing
c/o Canadian Manda Group, 165 Dufferin Street
Toronto, Ontario, Canada M6K 3H6
Distributed in the United Kingdom by GMC Distribution Services
Castle Place, 166 High Street, Lewes, East Sussex, England BN7 1XU
Distributed in Australia by Capricorn Link (Australia) Pty. Ltd.
P.O. Box 704, Windsor, NSW 2756, Australia

For information about custom editions, special sales, and premium and corporate
purchases, please contact Sterling Special Sales at 800-805-5489
or specialsales@sterlingpublishing.com.

Printed in China
Lot #:
2   4   6   8   10   9   7   5   3
04/13

www.sterlingpublishing.com/kids

SILVER PENNY STORIES

Snow White and the Seven Dwarfs

Told by Deanna McFadden
Illustrated by Jin Woo Kim

There once was a girl with skin as white as snow, lips as red as blood, and hair as black as ebony. Her mother named her Snow White.

When Snow White was still very young, her mother died. Her father remarried a beautiful woman who was secretly a wicked witch.

Snow White's stepmother insisted she was the prettiest woman in the kingdom. Every day, she stood in front of her magic mirror and asked: "Mirror, mirror, on the wall, who's the fairest of them all?"

The mirror always said: "You, O Queen, are the fairest of them all."

As time passed, Snow White grew prettier and prettier. One day, the queen stood before her mirror and asked, "Mirror, mirror, on the wall, who's the fairest of them all?"

This time the mirror said: "Snow White is the fairest in the land."

This made the queen very angry.

The queen ordered the kingdom's best hunter to take Snow White into the forest and kill her, returning with only her heart.

In the woods, the hunter took out his knife, but Snow White begged him for mercy.

The hunter took pity on the poor, sweet girl. Instead, he killed a wild boar and took its heart to the queen. He told her it was Snow White's heart.

Snow White ran through the forest until she came to a little cottage. When she stepped inside, she noticed that everything was tiny.

Seven small plates, seven small knives, and seven small forks were on the table. Seven tiny chairs were in the living room, and seven perfect little beds were in the bedroom. Not a spot of dust was anywhere.

Snow White tried each bed until she found one that was just right. She was so tired, and before she knew it, she was fast asleep.

Seven dwarfs lived in the cottage. As soon as they returned from their work in the mountains, they knew that someone was in their house. When the seventh dwarf looked at his bed, he found Snow White.

She looked so peaceful, the dwarfs didn't want to wake her.

In the morning, Snow White opened her eyes and saw all seven dwarfs staring at her. At first she was frightened.

"What is your name?" they asked. "And how have you come to our house?"

"I'm Snow White," she answered. She told them about her wicked stepmother.

The kind dwarfs said, "You may stay with us as long as you like, but you must promise not to let anyone inside the cottage."

The next day, the queen stood in front of her mirror, and the mirror said: "Snow White is hiding with seven dwarfs and is the fairest in the land."

The queen was angry. She raced to a secret part of the castle and made a poison apple.

Disguised as a poor peasant woman, the queen set off for the home of the seven dwarfs. When she arrived, she knocked on the door.

Snow White looked out the window, saw a poor peasant woman, and said, "I'm not allowed to let anyone in."

"But wouldn't you like this shiny red apple?" the queen asked, handing it to her through the open window.

The apple looked wonderful, so Snow White took a small bite. Immediately, she fell to the floor. A piece of poison apple was caught in her throat.

The queen laughed. Thinking Snow White was dead, she returned home to the castle and her magic mirror.

The seven dwarfs came home and found Snow White on the floor. They wept with grief.

The seven dwarfs couldn't bear to bury Snow White, because her cheeks were still rosy red and she looked so beautiful. Instead, they made her a glass coffin and took it to the top of the mountain. A dwarf always stayed by her side.

One day, a prince happened to ride by. When he saw Snow White in the glass coffin, he begged the dwarfs to let him bring her home to his kingdom. He thought he could help her. The dwarfs knew the prince was an honest and good man, so they said yes.

On the way down the mountain, the prince's horse stumbled over some rocks. The jolt freed the piece of poisoned apple from Snow White's throat.

Snow White sat up and said,
"Goodness, what happened?"

The prince was overjoyed to see Snow
White awake. He told her everything
and declared his love for her. Then he
asked for her hand in marriage.

The prince ordered his guards to capture the wicked stepmother. Then the prince and Snow White married. They lived happily ever after, and they had many joyful visits in the forest with the seven dwarfs.